Grandpa Loved

BY JOSEPHINE NOBISSO · ILLUSTRATED BY MAUREEN HYDE

Gingerbread House
Westhampton Beach, New York

Gingerbread House
602 Montauk Highway
Westhampton Beach
New York 11978

1 (631) 288-5119
Fax 1 (631) 288-5179
e-mail: ghbooks@optonline.net
www.gingerbreadbooks.com

Original version published by The Green Tiger Press
Subsequently published by Simon & Schuster
Gingerbread House SAN: 217-0760

Printed in Hong Kong
Manufactured by Regent Publishing Services Ltd.

Revised 2000
10 9 8 7 6 5 4 3 2 1

Publisher's Cataloging-in-Publication *(Provided by Quality Books, Inc.)*
Nobisso, Josephine.
Grandpa loved / by Josephine Nobisso;
illustrated by Maureen Hyde. -- 2nd ed.
p. cm.
SUMMARY: Grandpa's love of life insures that he
is still present, after his death, in the lives of all who loved
him.
LCCN: 99-75393
ISBN: 0-940112-04-3
1. Grandfathers--Juvenile fiction.
2. Grandfathers--Death--Juvenile fiction. 3. Death--Juvenile
fiction.
4. Grief in children--Juvenile fiction. 5. Bereavement in children--
Juvenile fiction.
I. Hyde, Maureen, ill. II. Title.

PZ7.N6645Gs 2000   [E]
                    QBI99-1372

To Grandpa Ralph and his four girls:
Nicolle, Gina, Bianca, and Kali Marie
—J.N.

For my father, with special thanks
to Russ, Jake and Sam.
—M.H.

Grandpa loved to stand on the beach.
He showed me how to love it, too.

We let the ocean foam creep up our legs, and the sun squint our eyes. We let the sea air breathe us–in and out, in and out–very deeply, very friendly.

Grandpa said that the earth was hurtling
through space so fast it sent winds
across the planet.

That's what Grandpa loved most about the beach–catching all that wind.

Grandpa loved the woods behind the summer house. He planted that love in me too.

We tumbled on soft moist moss, and tunneled into drifts of dry leaves.

We built a manger where deer and raccoons and birds came to eat our bread and corn and garden greens. Grandpa said that woodland creatures are so sensitive they can feel any nervousness around them.

That's what Grandpa loved most about the woods—being so calm and easy with all those animals.

Grandpa loved the city where we live. He taught me to love it, too. We let the dusty warm scent in museums carry us away, and the quiet buzz of the library lull us to doze.

We let any lost and lonely person tell us a life's story. Grandpa said that his being so old and my being so young made it easy for people to tell us so much.

That's what Grandpa loved most about
the city–hearing all those lives.

Grandpa loved the people in our family.
He grew that love in me, too.

We danced at weddings, and sang at parties. We played with the new babies, and visited the sick.

Grandpa said that people who died could go anywhere, at any time. That must be what Grandpa loves most now–being with us everywhere, all the time–on the beach, in the country, and in the city–in the lives of all who loved him.